FAVOURITE NURSERY RHYMES

Published by Top That! Publishing plc
Tide Mill Way, Woodbridge, Suffolk, IP12 1AP, UK
www.topthatpublishing.com
Copyright © 2013 Top That! Publishing plc
All rights reserved
0 2 4 6 8 9 7 5 3 1
Printed and bound in China

Creative Director – Simon Couchman
Editorial Director – Daniel Graham

Illustrated by Alison Atkins

ISBN 978-1-78244-002-4

A catalogue record for this book is available from the British Library
Printed and bound in China

Humpty Dumpty

Humpty Dumpty
sat on a wall,

Humpty Dumpty
had a great fall,

All the king's horses
and all the king's men,

Couldn't put Humpty
together again.

Little Bo Peep

Little Bo Peep
has lost her sheep,
And doesn't know
where to find them.
Leave them alone
and they'll come home,
Bringing their tails
behind them.

Jack and Jill

Jack and Jill
went up the hill,
To fetch a pail of water,
Jack fell down
and broke his crown,
And Jill came
tumbling after.

Little Miss Muffet

Little Miss Muffet
sat on her tuffet,
Eating her curds and whey,
Along came a spider,
And sat down beside her,
And frightened
Miss Muffet away.

Mary, Mary

Mary, Mary
quite contrary,

How does
your garden grow?

With silver bells
and cockle shells,

And pretty maids
all in a row.

Hic!

Incy Wincy Spider

Incy Wincy Spider
Climbed up the water spout,

Down came the rain
and washed poor Incy out,

Out came the sun
and dried up all the rain,

Incy Wincy Spider
climbed up the spout again.

Mary had a Little Lamb

Mary had a little lamb,
its fleece was white as snow,
And everywhere that Mary went
the lamb was sure to go.

It followed her to school one day,
which was against the rule.

It made the children
laugh and play
to see a lamb at school.

Baa, Baa, Black Sheep

Baa, baa, black sheep,
have you any wool?

Yes sir, yes sir,
three bags full.

One for the master,
one for the dame,

And one for the little boy
who lives down the lane.

Little Jack Horner

Little Jack Horner,
sat in a corner,
Eating his Christmas pie,
He put in his thumb
and pulled out a plum,
And said
'What a good boy am I'.

Hey, Diddle, Diddle

Hey, diddle, diddle,

The cat and the fiddle,

The cow jumped
over the moon.

The little dog laughed
to see such fun,

And the dish ran away
with the spoon.